SUZY AND SAMMY

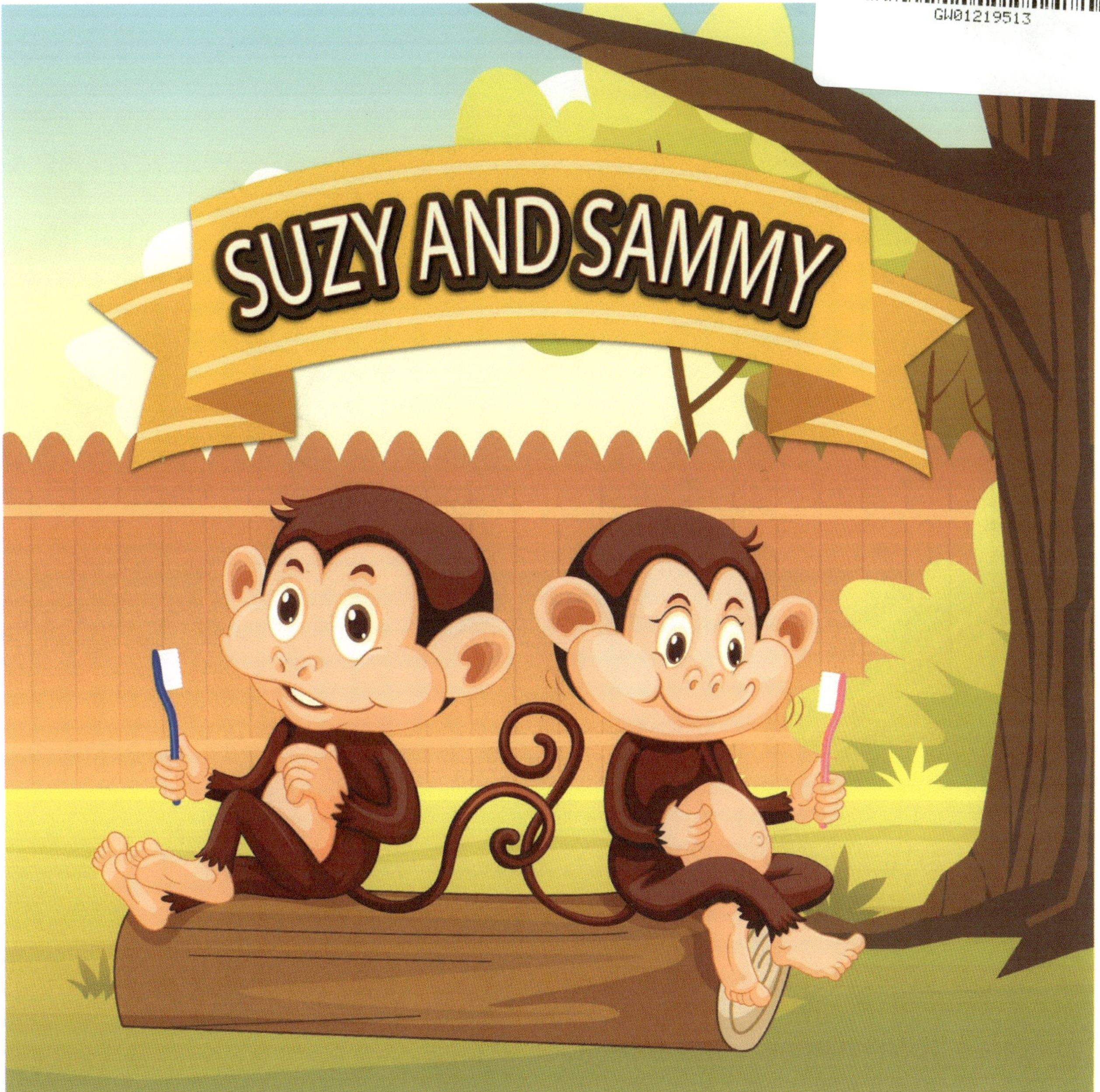

Suzy and Sammy look at each other. Sammy then looks down at his toothbrush and dropping his toothbrush yells ………….

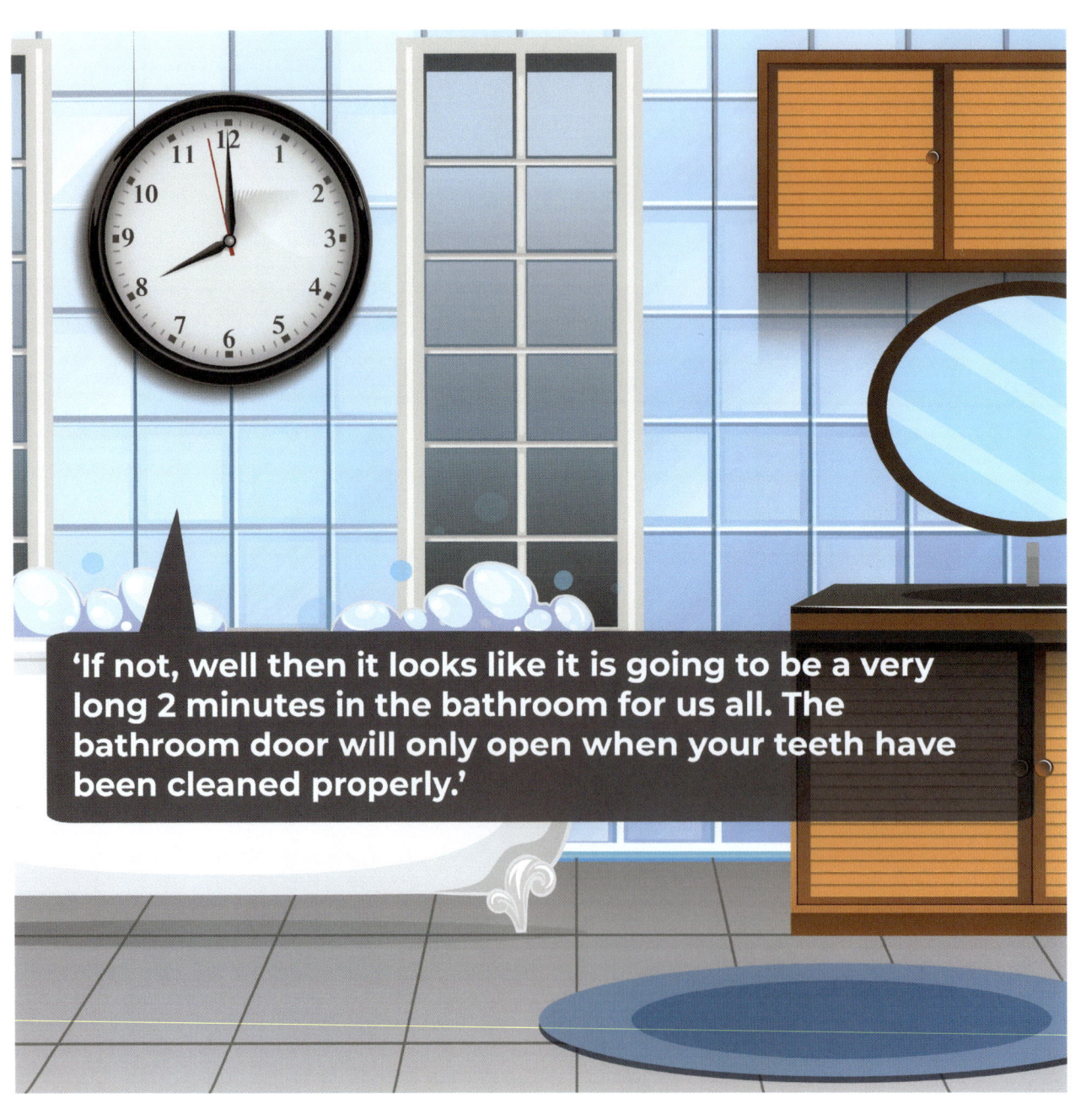

'If not, well then it looks like it is going to be a very long 2 minutes in the bathroom for us all. The bathroom door will only open when your teeth have been cleaned properly.'

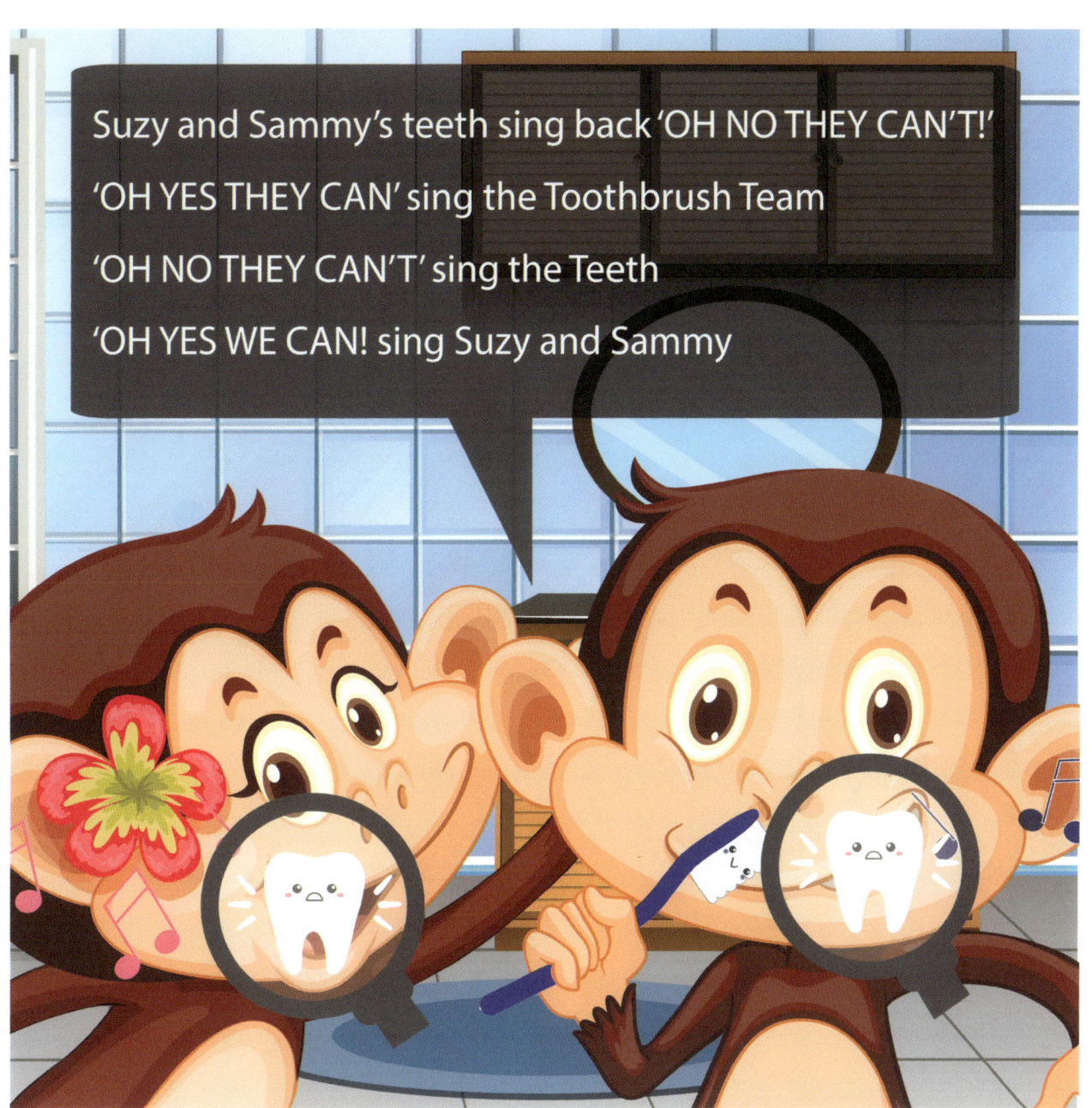

Suzy and Sammy now feel brave and they pick up their new toothbrushes. The toothpaste helps them put a pea size amount of toothpaste on their brushes and then they prepare themselves to join in and learn the rest of the song.

Mummy tells them she has a letter from the Dentist to read to them before they sleep. The letter says:

Dear Suzy and Sammy, I hope you are both well and are enjoying your new magical toothbrushes. I am sure by now your teeth are happy and that you are practicing the Toothbrush Song. I cannot wait to see you and ……………

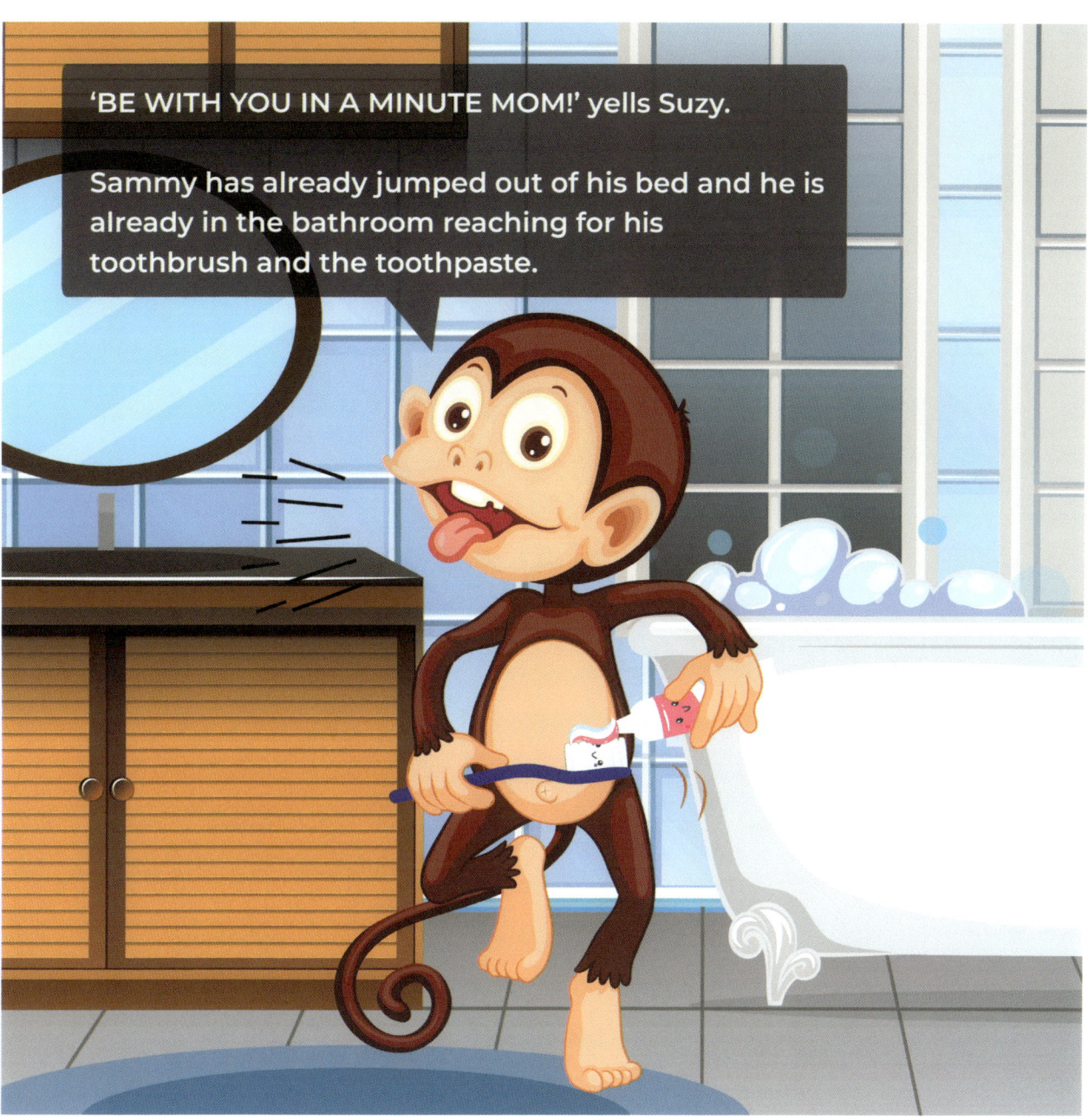

Printed in Great Britain
by Amazon